Pig Gets Lost

Heather Amery

Illustrated by Stephen Cartwright

Language consultant: Betty Root
Series editor: Jenny Tyler

There is a little yellow duck to find on every page.

This is Apple Tree Farm.

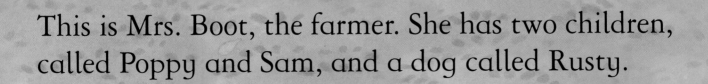

This is Mrs. Boot, the farmer. She has two children, called Poppy and Sam, and a dog called Rusty.

Mrs. Boot has six pigs.

There is a mother pig and five baby pigs.
The smallest pig is called Curly. They live in a pen.

Mrs. Boot feeds the pigs every morning.

She takes them two big buckets of food.
But where is Curly? He is not in the pen.

She calls Poppy and Sam.

"Curly's gone," she says. "I need your help to find him."

"Where are you, Curly?"

Poppy and Sam call to Curly. "Let's look in the hen run," says Mrs. Boot. But Curly is not there.

"There he is, in the barn."

"He's in the barn," says Sam. "I can just see his tail." They all run into the barn to catch Curly.

"That's not Curly."

"It's only a piece of rope," says Mrs. Boot. "Not Curly's tail." "Where can he be?" says Poppy.

"Maybe he's eating the cows' food."

But Curly is not with the cows. "Don't worry," says Mrs. Boot. "We'll soon find him."

"Perhaps he's in the garden."

They look for Curly in the garden, but he is not there. "We'll never find him," says Sam.

"Why is Rusty barking?"

Rusty is standing by a ditch. He barks and barks.
"He's trying to tell us something," says Poppy.

"Rusty has found Curly."

They all look in the ditch. Curly has slipped down into the mud and can't climb out.

"We'll have to lift him out."

"I'll get into the ditch," says Mrs. Boot. "I'm coming too," says Poppy. "And me," says Sam.

Curly is very muddy.

Mrs. Boot picks Curly up but he struggles. Then
he slips back into the mud with a splash.

Now everyone is very muddy.

Sam tries to catch Curly but he falls into the mud.
Mrs. Boot grabs Curly and climbs out of the ditch.

They all climb out of the ditch.

"We all need a good bath," says Mrs. Boot.
"Rusty found Curly. Clever dog," says Sam.

Cover design by Hannah Ahmed   Digital manipulation by Natacha Goransky

This edition first published in 2004 by Usborne Publishing Ltd, 83-85 Saffron Hill, London EC1N 8RT, England. www.usborne.com
Copyright © 2004, 1989 Usborne Publishing Ltd. The name Usborne and the devices ♀ ☺ are Trade Marks of Usborne Publishing Ltd. All rights reserved.
No part of this publication may be reproduced, stored in a retrieval system, or transmitted in any form or by any means, electronic, mechanical, photocopying,
recording or otherwise, without prior permission of the publisher. UE. This edition first published in America in 2004. Printed in China.